AF322590

THE ABANDONED POET

SARIN ARYAL

About the Book

Life is simple, we humans are complicated. It's all about the words. The same gift named "Word" that boomed and doomed the humanity. This is a book consisting of Poems that has been derived from the Pain, Agony, love/betrayal, Sanity/ Insanity, happiness/sadness, and overall experience of life penned down together.

P.S. All these poems have been written under 7 minutes (each) in a free write session.

About the Writer

Who Am I?

A man lost in his own world? A dreamer? A believer? Well, I would like to think of myself as a Zero. "An Oblivion".

My human name is Sarin Aryal and I was born and raised in this vessel in a beautiful city named Kathmandu, in a beautiful country Nepal. Kathmandu happens to be the mystical city of temples. You heard that right, there is a temple for every block in this city. I am currently based in California, the city of tech. There is an irony to that, as techs are the new temples, there is a tech temple for every block in these streets of Silicon Valley. I did my bachelor's in civil engineering, then I switched to a different God named IT. By profession I am now a software engineer. But I would like to call myself a mere Poet and a musician. This book is not just about a collection of poems. Every word I pour into these poems is from all the experiences I have gathered, lived, and suffered on this planet from the past 3 decades. I hope these words resonates in your heart and soul. Oh, and I am obsessed with number 3. Namaste

I would like to thank my family and Special Thanks to my friends, motivators, and biggest source of inspiration:

- Lady TJ Curl
- David Lee Hawks
- Hannah Brennan
- Hope Anderson
- Sam Iwata aka Liu
- PJ Galati
- Jill Flakne
- Sarah Kezman

TABLE OF CONTENTS

MOLLY

Molly was a day away from being eighteen,
got groomed in a fresh pair of leather by her maiden
It was supposed to be the day for her to awaken
Little did she know; this night was about to get shaken
Monster's claws upon her body, her innocence was taken

He lured, grinned, scratched, ripped off her clothes
And forced himself upon her body
She froze, cried, begged, shouted
Screamed for help, no one around to defend her body

Molly was not alone living this nightmare, there were others
She died every morning gazing into the shameful eyes of her mother
Here comes another day where her old man can't afford to get sober
She must make peace with the grief coz no one else bother

Molly woke up late one day, sun was about to set
A bird flew by her window with white and shiny feathers
A difficult decision was made on that gloomy weather
She sanctioned her own execution, wearing that same pair of leather
Molly whispered "to be hanged till death"
A difficult decision was made coz nobody bothered.

CIVIL WAR

There is nothing Civil about the civil war
They give you guns to acquire those paper bills and golden bars
They use you, play you, slay you and lock you up in a prison bar
They make your Soul wounded and leave you with a scar
There is nothing civil about the civil war

Chaos everywhere, there is no running from the faith
Hot metal .49 chasing you down to the journey of death
The pile of bodies unattended outside the cemetery gate
They put a blame on you for all the deaths
The old art of thought control convincing your every breath
"What we have here is failure to communicate"

MY FRIEND NAMED GUITAR

You are my coffee in the morning
And my chill in the evening
You are my offence in rage
And my defense when I hide myself inside my inner cage

You be my Baritone in gloomy days
My soprano when I am parting ways
Your melodies are everything my words failed to say
You are a shimmering light when the black clouds are covering Apollo's
ray

I am playing defense
I am surrendering to you
Blisters of burn inside my heart
words I got are very few

You are my coffee in the morning
My chill in the evening
I am surrendering myself; you are the ointment to my scar and class to
my cigar
My Rose wood textured melodic blend; my loyal friend named Guitar

A LETTER TO MY EX

You said you want another chance
Well sorry honey, this ship has been sailed
Sailed a long time ago and all those memories are jailed
Nothing will have effect anymore, it can no longer be bailed

I despised you and hated you
But those are also feelings, so I had to stop
Your tears remind me of an ocean
You know salt triggers the wound even with a single drop

I am not spell bound by your faded charm anymore
You can shoot me with any sentimental arsenal in store
The only nation you and I will be together is moderation
When it comes to you, I prefer to rest my case without consideration

THE ABANDONED POET

Here comes the story of a broken man
Nights are cold and days are hard
The circle of life feeds on his consciousness
He sleeps in an abandoned van

He is an abandoned poet, but one day he is going to make it
They curse, swear and spits as he limps
He smiles as if nothing bothers him
What a great man, how easily he can fake it

People dream about wealth and material selection
And make their self-existence harsh
He dreams about energy and spirits, that's his natural selections
Lost within the galactic wings dreaming about Jupiter and Mars

There goes the story of a broken man
Nights were cold and days were hard
Staring at the picture of van hanging to his bedroom wall
No more crawling of bugs, no more hissing of mouse
Broken junks and all those rusty dreams helped him to shape his house

WHAT IF?

What if you are in a video game?
And you are the player that's just lame
The one that always gives up
The one that's too easy to tame

What if God coded you in his opponents' image?
And you misunderstood the process with superstitious rage
What if homo sapiens are the programmed descendant of devil?
What if darkness is Good and light is evil?

What if the server goes down?
And the world just stops
You are eating your lunch
And your head just pops?

What if you are on a short trip?
In someone else's digital limbo
The sound vibrations are the actual commands
And the languages are just mumbo jumbo

What if you are in a video game?
And you are the player that's just lame
You wasted your time pursuing luxury just to be in top of your game
Now your juice is running out
The operation or the operator whom do you blame?
What if this game got no mushrooms?
It won't give you options to revive
What if your dreams are the saved progress?
This a matrix and you only have a minute to survive.

A SINGLE DIME

Once upon a time
I wrote a rhyme
Composed some melodies that chyme
Dreamed about recording but my net worth was a single dime

I hated that dime
I hated that time
My mind was flooded with ideas
Barely survived club 27 I was on my prime

All those rejections
Financial declines
I hated that dime
I hated that time

I knew I could make it
But didn't know how
I didn't like it then
but I love it now

THE HANGED MAN RESOLUTIONS

He hanged his luck and hanged his faith
In a pool of sorrow, he drank and bathe
He hanged his smile and cursed his faith
In a pool of guilt, deception, and regrets

He hanged his love and hanged his stress
He hanged his resolution in a pool of distress
He hanged his wrath and hanged his gain
He hanged his absolution in a pool of pain

One hell of a man he was
He hanged his goal
Hanged his goal and hanged his dream
hanged himself in a cynical stream

THE SANITY SONG

Behold your senses here comes the greatest story
Story about crazy Jim and the sanity he is about to bury
Jim lives in the world where mental health is a taboo, a curse one carries
Trust me when I say this, insanity is innocence & sanity is scary

Jim often gets series of anxiety
And it comes in different variety
Tik-Tok; here comes the moment, Jim is gasping for breath again
Hyperventilating lying on his knees, one more crazy act for the society

Take a Look at yourself in someone else's story; you, yes you are a dork
Open your arms for the man, its easy if you try,
Come on you insanely sane people what it takes is just a little teamwork
Verbal diarrhea and spitting out names
That's the real insanity you better change your game

This story will change your life; don't just listen, comprehend
Well, you see every broken heart can be mend
Mental health is a song that nobody wants to sing
Let me do the honor and sing you a song straight out of my dream
Hey there crazy world, I am Jim you are Jim, we all are Jim

PURE JOY

Isn't it too early for beer?
Who cares, I'll just float some cereals in it
I normally gargle with Listerine
But Tequila's not bad for it

I only drink on two special days
The day that rains and the day that doesn't
Vulnerable heart witnessed the ploy
Bottle of ethanol lodged in my head, that's my definition of pure joy

SHANGHAI

I am in this cold room in California
Holding my guitar sipping my rye
Thinking about my muse
She is back in Shanghai

Staring at her picture in my favorite ripped jeans
I mounted it on my wall using the dart
The same dart that resembles the airplane
The same airplane I wish to board someday
Leaving behind all these miles apart

I am holding this cheap, close but no Cigar
Cloud of smokes cursing my fate
My muse back in Shanghai cursing her fate
Windy and chilly my body is cold
First time I saw her my heart got sold

I am accompanied by this loneliness
Holding my guitar sipping my rye
Eyes longing for my muse that was a painful goodbye
She is gracefully showering her warmth
Longing for me back in Shanghai.

FATHER

For all my wrongs that let you down
For all your dreams that was blown
Father, I thank you for making me your own
Thank you for my first pencil and my first phone
Thank you for that first guitar, I owe you all my tone

For all my rights that made you proud
I am Sorry for all those pettifoggery when I was stupid and loud
Father, I thank you for being my shelter during the stormy cloud
So grateful I am to call myself your blood
Thank you for the man I am, and for all the applaud

SON

Son, comprehend the words I am about to tell
Redemption from being an arrogant person
That's something I will never buy, and you can never sell
Pay attention son for the things I am about to tell

Let me take you on a path
A path intersecting evil and good
A path full of wrath
That's clouding your judgement and consuming your manhood

Be good to all, for this will be your only life
No mistress waiting for you in the afterlife
Heaven and hell both are here
The journey to the light is far and darkness is near

Don't mess things up then come to me and complain
There is nothing in your words that makes me entertain
Now eat your food and shut your trap
Be good son, it's time for me to nap

THE THEATER OF THE ABSURD

Its wonderful tonight Clapton filling all my void
I am comfortably numb surrounded by the sound waves of pink Floyd
There will be a tequila sunrise Eagles said that right
Metallica's giving you that one pointer
You better be ready for the fight

I wish I had the poetry of Morrison
And strumming of Jack Johnson
666 is the number of the beast
Wish I had the trooper like Bruce Dickinson

My stereo is loud, records are stacked up forming a layer
Can't get over with heart break warfare listening to John Mayer
Can't imagine that crash replicating the lyrics of free bird
Wolfmother narrating Joker and the thief
BB King singing his heart out about Lucille
I am trapped in the theater of absurd.

BAD TO THE BONES

Weary and tired
Here I am in my country attire
Pack of long horn in my back pocket
Got my baby's picture in this bronze locket

Oh, Baby I am bad
I am bad to the bones
Had to make some tough calls
Needed to unturn some stones

Playing my records, sipping a bourbon by the fire
It's a cold and long night you are what heart desire
Been moving places with boxes full of memories
coming home to you mama, she is going to put me out of my miseries

Oh, Baby I am bad
I am bad to the bones
Had to make some tough calls
Needed to unturn some stones

DON'T MAKE ME MEAN

Do you remember the last November?
The November full of rain
The rain that's weeping from the sky
The weeping of all the agony and pain

The pain of my countless children
My children with branches and leaves
The leaves that shelter you was all in vain
You ungraceful humans had all those tricks up on your sleeves

I warn you to stop; don't make me mean
Don't make me mean, I will wipe you clean
wipe your existence to the very core
you witnessed my anger but have barely seen what's in the store
the store is full of disaster, and you won't be feeling the Sun
you won't be feeling the Sun or witness the moon anymore

MR. KING

Hello Mr. King, where is your crown?
Where is your staff that you hold full of ego and frown?
Where is your kingdom surrounded by the hungry town?
All the verbal diarrhea you throw out regardless of verbs, adjectives, or
nouns.

Hello Mr. King, we meet again
Your castle crumbled and I can see your pain
Did you listen to the bard songs about the wrath and vain?
Or did you listen to those love songs that shackles your rib caged heart
in a chain?

Bye Mr. King the sun is down, now the moons comes with a rain
I hope you find your peace after all this time of being insane.
I bid you farewell, time to get rid of your cloak and that masculine mane
Roads are filthy and the journey is long; don't forget to carry your cane.

BARD SONG

The nostalgic smell of country grass
I can hear a bard singing his songs
Strumming his guitar in the woods
Playing with his messy hair reflecting on all the poor choices and all the
wrongs

The chorus says "life is all about the journey"
We halt and move forward like a travelling bus
All we must do is to decide which stop we choose to explore
And what to do with the time given to us

The smell of country grass
The logs of freshly chopped trees
Piling up in my yard resonating my doings
The bard song helped me find my ground
Brought me into my knees.

MY BIGGEST FEAR MY ANGER

There was a time
Day was cold and sun didn't shine
You got into my nerves
I acted fine

There was a time
I had a song, but it didn't rhyme
You took advantage of me while I was starving
I didn't have a single dime

You pushed my limit
I knew you'd pay
If not today
This grudge will consume you some day

Don't get into my nerves
Because I have a fear
I won't be the man you see now dear
When my fear possesses me, I don't want you near.

There was a time
Night was dark and moon didn't shine
You awakened my fear
Behold the consequence that even words can't define.

THE BUGS IN MY BRAIN

The bugs in my brain crawling in at night
Once again holding this pillow, trying to suppress the fight
Done many wrongs, finding a way to make things right
Being still in this vessel, my soul is demanding a flight

Breathing in and breathing out
On Countless nights I curse and shout
Tears fall, eyes are swelled
Dwelling in the land of drought

The bugs in my brain crawling in at night
Darkness all over, no sign of a shimmering light
Now I see what's wrong, and ready to make it right
Everything I had been searching, was right before my eyes

THE TRANSISTOR TRILOGY

i. Transistor

I got all the things that was listed
Was about to complete the puzzle
But the transistor was twisted
Better hide it before I get knocked down
As you see there was a time I had been fisted
Man, my chief is cruel, 200 light years passed, and I was completely
wasted
30 minutes before this gigantic ship's launch
Maybe this shiny looking wire works, I have a hunch
He is not looking I better hurry, dimensions are open we are about to
jump
Set the course on the dashboard, thrust is open and lever is ready to
pump

I reached to the wire replacing the transistor
A shadow behind me yelling, what you doing mister?
Don't put it in there, you maggot, you are lucky I caught you in an act
of disaster
Your future's uncertain boy and the end is always near
That's the ignition for my blaster
They are supposed to be the way they are, you clumsy bastard
We would have been toasted in cold dark space
If it wasn't for that twisted transistor

ii. Vessel

The twisted transistors, electrons emitting the spark.
It's cold and chilly up here, tranquility within the dark
I am looking at the blue sphere, leaning on to this space station's poles.
They said space is just a void with space junks and multiple black holes

Maybe this was it, maybe this was the place for my vessel to park
Far from the chaos I found the profound happiness within the dark
Not a single entity around no cosmic bodies and their spark
I knew within my soul; this was the place for my vessel to park

iii. Grounded

Debris all over, black smoke and I am surrounded
Ejecting my capsule, folks pulled me out and now I am grounded
Something is ringing in my head, well loud was what that sounded
Fire everywhere, Teary eyes and I am Surrounded

Mayday was the last thing I shouted
Well, that transistor was twisted for a reason when this station was founded
That spark was a death sentence, nowhere to run or hide I am bounded
Is this hell or is this a heaven? My mind and soul are clouded.

TELL ME

There is only one life left what do you do brother?
Will you drink yourself to death or you going to act sober
Tell me if life came with fixed expiry date
Would you still roam places trying to find different mates?

The peroxide is already wrinkling you just after you were born
Would you still be interested to see your unborn?
Tell me if life came with fixed expiry date
Would you still tangle yourself in misogyny, racism, and religious hate?

Would you still try to act God?
Would you still be searching where the party is popping?
Would you still be trapped in your emotional pod?
Any day now you might be buried or cremated to ashes; will that be all?
Is there no reason for hoping?

WHEN I WAS A CHILD

When I was a kid, life was easy with full of adventurous act
As they say, broken knees are easy to fix than the broken heart
Sweating in playground, merry goes round and round
McDonald knew nothing about politics he just had a farm with
goodness around
Slowly I found, tying the shoelaces is not as complicated as it sounds

I have lived last 2 decades just paying my bills
The Longer I live, the more uninformed I feel
chaos, anxiety, depression, and grief are the only thing adult life will ever
bring
I feel only the young have an explanation for everything

When I was a child, life was fun full of excitement
As I grew older the only thing that remains is resentment
It was easy to trust and bloom a flora of attachment
No, not anymore, it's all about deceiving and detachment
The longer I live the more uninformed I feel
only the young have an explanation for everything.

YOU ARE FINALLY HOME

Once upon a time underneath the vortex
There was a man with mighty neocortex
He was born a Pegan, blessed with unusual context
Observing the spherical pattern all around him including the vortex

He had this muse high above the fire
Born with a single faith but millions of desires
She was trying so hard to make her heard
Her heart and soul were constantly on obsessed emotions of pyre

Fire and ice we chase, and we roam
I pray in the mountains, you pray on dorm
Beyond all the measures and social norm
I am holding you, just breath and don't fear the storm
Because my love you are finally home

THE KATHMANDU SUNSHINE

I am surrounded by green in this majestic vine
Waiting for my dawn, the sun is about to shine
Playing my six strings in this city of temples
The melody sounds so fine

The shadow of this pagodas
Painting these streets in colors of shade
Body fusing with this early morning droplets
Lying in this cold muddy bed

When you are all alone, you think about
a companion that goes well with wine and dine
Waiting for my dawn in this street of Kathmandu
Beholding my heart, for the sun is about to shine.

A MEMORY THAT WAS NOT YOURS

I woke up full of sweat and heat
I can feel the pounding of my heartbeat
It's 3 AM and I am cursing that clock again
Hoping for someone to show me the way so this mental rush can be
blocked and chained

The yearning and the wrath I must endure with this curse
But today it was a bit different right before I was awake someone was
narrating a verse
Heard a voice saying "let me take you to a mystical tour deep inside that
brain of yours"
Listen Son this is what supposed to feel when you are dreaming a
memory that was not yours.

LUCIFER BLUES

Boy, I heard you made a deal
you made a deal at the crossroad
You sold your soul
Sold it to the devil

I heard you let your guitar got loose
And accepted the music that devil choose
I heard you were playing the tritone, the note that devil choose
You pray for Satan through your music fooling us by calling it blues

If you play your music in reverse, they are the Satan's verse
Chorus filled with dark magic, language very remorse
They say you wear a robe at night and ride a headless horse
Even your family disowned you and closed their door

Behold for the punishment that you are about to get
Even my church can't save you from your hideous fate
Spiritus Sanctus, even the exorcism doesn't work
Your heart is shallow, and your soul has been pierced by devil's fork

Old man, I may be out of breath, but I am hearing you fine
You just killed a son of God in his very house
Hallowed be thy name old man, you just crossed the line
Remember this day on a death bed when your tab is about to close
I'll be welcoming you in the afterlife playing my lucifer blues

A TRIBUTE FOR MY DOGS (IN LOVING MEMORY OF BROWNIE AND PUNTE)

I am watching your picture again
Submerging into this river of pain
My opinions are vague
All I can think about is agony and rage
The soothing bark of yours is ringing in my head
Keeping your memory alive with this music full of happiness and tears.

A part of me died along with you, when I can no longer feel you aside my bed
A part of me died when I can find no more of the hairs you shed
I am writing this tribute in your memories which can never fade
The wagging of your tail and that starry eyes is playing in a loop inside my head

IMPRISONED

In this crowd followed by loneliness
Wrath in the eyes, heart filled with emptiness
Imprisoned by your own sanity
In this darkness of abusiveness
One two and three, each step you take leading to anxiousness
Dirt in your hand, pounding of heart with restlessness
Caged in your own thoughts, no room for righteousness
Men like you from ages, suffered from this absence of mindfulness

ASH TO ASH, DUST TO DUST

The glares in my eyes
The race between heart and mind always seems to tie
Dust to dust, ash to ash now watch me rise
Watch me levitate like the kites in the sky
I died thousand deaths; all I need is one cardioversion to wave goodbye

When its real good but also bad
When it makes you euphoric but also sad
See those glare in my eyes
Feel the pounding of my heart
The rushing in my cerebellum, the thoughts are about to die
Ash to ash, dust to dust, now watch me rise
I was bad to the bones
Witnessed the diabolic darkness that creeps and crawls on you until it
dies

WHY?

No one can hear you scream
Pool of blood flowing down the stream
This is a war my friend
Comes with a promise and ends up breaking all the dreams

Men in heavy boots and morphine
Gunpowder Traded by one little sound Gathered in team
Broken arms and severed limbs
Collateral damage all over; so much for your fairy dream

Why do the leaders fight the war?
Why do they always send the poor?
Why do they always drop the key in a crucial moment?
Why do they always shut the door?

Guns and cannon balls
Dusted earth and severed walls
Gasping for breath
One more step closer to death

They feed you lies from the table clothe
Hunting tigers controlled by big belly sloth
Pool of blood flowing down the stream
This is a war my friend it shatters all you dream

THE VAMPIRE

The blinking of your radiant eyes
As tranquil as the sky
The melody of your voice
My heart stopped for a second, I am full of rejoice

Is this the dress that's making you pretty?
Or it's the other way around?
My head goes round and round and round
You have me spell bound

The blinking of your eyes
Uplifting my emotional tides
Can't get out in the sunlight
Just invite me in and I Will make it up to you every night
I was once a man with urges for blood, violence, and riots
I am waving a white flag to your elegance, I surrender my existential
fight

THE THOUGHTS THAT CRAWL

The thoughts that crawl
The regrets that growl
The game we play as foul
The tangling web of Black widow on a roll
The mind is empty the sense in the skin is null

Heart pounding
Eyes are tired and weary
Not fully awake not sleep sounding
The thoughts that crawl
The Regrets that growl

THE MORE I

Something shiny something warm
The ray of sun inside this metal barn
The flourishing bud
On top of this aromatic mud

I have been high, I have been low
Playing the violin holding this mighty bow
The concert is over, but the music just started
Playing the Cadenza for the moments we met and departed
Something shiny something warm
The ray of sun inside this metal barn
Something at my sight
Giving me a will to fight

The more I grieve
The more I learn
For all the wrong
And for all the right

THE FAME (LAST SUPPER)

I never cared for fame
Never knew how to play this game
Can't stand this so-called luxurious cult
Can't be a part of this mass revolt

Women made of paper
Men made of clay
Fragile and sophisticated
Wrapped with colors and glitters
Out there on the spotlight getting ready to slay

You can have all the sushi you want
But you struggle to hold your chopstick
Pork ribs, raw livers, tablecloth, and fancy cutter
Six feet under, surrounded by dirt and heavy brick
Eventually you yourself is going to be the last supper

WHEN I WAS YOUNG

This is not a fairy tale
It's merely a song about survival
The ending doesn't end with redemption
It's barely a revival

Chains and leather, smokes and McBeth
Gasoline and motorcycles, that smell of death
Candlelight and aluminum foil
Zippo and flame, spoon full of powder that boils

When I was young, I was the king of the world
Like a moth into the flame, thrill was all I cheered, and the life was bold
This is a tale about a puppy with no hungry belly and no bills to pay
Never asked for feedbacks, never cared what the world would say

This is not a fairy tale
It's merely a song about survival
The ending doesn't end here
It's just another revival

A PATH IN A SNOW

She wanted a king, I was a dark knight
She wanted colors, golds, glitters, and sunlight
I was made of dirt, cold, darkness, and moonlight
She wanted someone extravagant who would take her to different sights
I was just a simple man, all I could do for her was struggle, sweat, protect and fight

Look at us now
How many sights have you seen so far?
The day you left me I lost one battle
But honey since then I haven't lost a single war
Tell me are you still self-composed? Are those emotions still cold and remorse?
Are you still taking a path in a snow?
A huntress with arrow of betrayal accompanied by ruthless bow

Tell me, was it worth it to chase fantasies all your life?
Trying desperate measures to be the queen of your self-proclaimed hive
Do you cry yourself a river when no one's around?
Is this what you meant when you said you wish for a different life than mine?

SMOKES AND MIRRORS

Smokes and Mirrors
Night full of terror
Howling in the wind, it's about that time
My heart kick starts like an old rusty turbine

Is it yet another magic engraved in my genes?
Or is it passed down by my ancestors who were a living machine
Is it a blind faith I have in God that's pumping my insanity?
Or is it a disgrace I find, in all of humanity

Dusty windows and rusty gate
No more belief in tranquil fate
No more magic or pixies tagged along
One more revolution of blue sphere and yet I am all alone

THE ROOM

He was there, lying-in pool of blood
Scissors engraved deep in his veins
No one could ever imagine what was his pain
But you see, action speaks louder than word

The room was full of tools and boy it was cold
The axe he used to carry all the time
He was convinced it made him bold
Cordless drills and all those thrills
Those days were gold

I bid you farewell my friend
This vessel was a real fun
I bid you farewell my friend
Someone is calling me from the beyond

FORBIDDEN GARDEN

Limes and lemons
Angels and demons
Standing in this forbidden garden
Holding this apple with a heavy heart and shoulder full of burden

Kings and sage
Hatred and rage
A Bottle of Stout, my loyal companion while seeding these Brussels
sprouts
I am pulling out this tomato holding the roots
Is it a vegetable or is it some fruit?

I asked the King, he shut me down
I asked the sage he puzzled me around
I got lost and confused tasting these apricots
The Deeper the roots higher the thoughts

Smokes and mirrors
Clouds and amber
Dragon fruits and cucumber
This is a moment to remember

MY DRUG NAMED SANE

I once fell in love
her complexion was white
hard from the outside
But once I caress, she was smooth and fine

Devoured her faint smokey soul through my mouth
Sniffed her body, quenched my thirst no more drought
My lips were hard, and tongue was numb
In love and naive, wild but dumb

She loved to spread her wings near the glasses and mirrors
Took me to a happy place, no wrath, agony no more horrors
No more pain no reason to sought
You, me, a card, and few dollar bills that's what life was about

Changed my coordinates, no more navigation to the sea of gram
No more of Benjamins rolled with a charm
I broke up with her and many winters have passed
in her direction I am no more compassed

No more of the anxious night
No bugs in my brain, dwelling and asking for the fight
No runny nose no more pain
My beloved ex, my muse, my drug named sane.

IN THIS REALM

I live in this realm
Where truth breed lies
I live in this realm
Where miscommunications end up as goodbyes

You live in your world, and I do in mine
Your porcelain skin no more makes my heart rhyme
Having to repeat myself from time to time
Your memories are fading to black
No glimpse of hope no more sunshine

I live in this realm
Where truth breed lies
You crashed your world, and I crashed mine
You carry your burden and I carry mine

AGONY OF SUPERMAN

My solitude of fortress
Witnessed all my stress
I wear this symbol of hope
But inside I am naked, my heart full of distress

I tried to be in your shoes
And you tried mine
We both tried hard
It didn't fit us right

We came across this land
A land between streams
You were there with full of rage
I with shattered dreams

I suppressed my urges
And shouldered all your fight
You still couldn't trust me and shattered my heart
Shattered my heart with a kryptonite

SEEING THINGS CLEARLY

I was blinded once
Warrior armed with shields and spears
Bathe in the pool of blood
No one to hold on to, no reason to shed tears

They called me, "Death riding the horse"
Name widespread, full of terrors and fear
A sinner once a sinner twice
Gambling life rolling my dice

Until the moment I couldn't lead anymore
At that moment, all those victories were remorse
I am in a death row
Now my vision is clear
There is no end for this hunger
The power lasted a minute, suffering is longer

DARK TRANQUILITY

Trapped inside this turmoil of hate
We all are dying since the day we are born
Gone were the days of kindness, everyone and everything is torn
We all are born with indigenous debt tattooed to our fate

Restrained to this dark tranquility within yourself
Naive thoughts and mediocre skills won't help you get far
Blunt Emotions trying to connect families seems as remorse as reaching
the star
Chained inside this wall of lies, waging war within your true self

THE MAN AND THE YOUNG MAN

Hey there young man
A voice resonates
Walls shaking a shock wave detonates
Who are you good sir? Asked the man
I am only a travelling guide he replied
I am here to haul your soul in a memory van

Where am I travelling asked the young fellow?
Well to the land where sun is warm, and the drinks are mellow
But I don't have a ticket and I can't see no stall
Don't worry my child, you don't need a ticket
Just stand by that brightly colored wall.

Hidden beneath the steams I saw one tire
Is this my ride? Oh, good sire?
Yes, my son said the man
Grab any seat your soul desire.

POURING OUT

That heart is never pouring out
That stain is never getting out
The wrath, agony, and pain
Those screams and curses that we each gain
The way we stopped talking and all we did was shout
That stain is never getting out

Well, I tried different keys
But the locks were lost underneath those emotional sprout
I tried once and twice and then I lost the count
Never enough for you regardless of whatever may be the amount
Eyes are cold and lack of emotion I behold
This heart is never pouring out
This stain is never getting out

GAMBLE

The world is a big old casino my friend
We gamble to survive
Decks cut in half, fingers tingling to foreplay the card
We empty our pocket each night to bed, in a hope to revive

Tables laid on top of a briar patch
A flamboyant dealer shutting the bet with a golden latch
This ambient with gin and tonic
Listen closely, even the chaos sounds too harmonic

In this giant slot machine
Someone else is pulling the bar
The cut so deep that pierce your soul
leaving you with a lifelong scar

AN AWARENESS OF GHOST

It's 3 Am at night or morning if you will
The room is damp and cold; it's giving me a chill
Shadows and voices, let's start this fight
I am feeling the presence but nothing's on my sight

Am I going crazy or it's just a play?
A play of my mind where my consciousness getting slayed
Am I going color blind? Coz all I see is red
As red as my blood dripping down the blade

Am I hallucinating, or the existence is real?
Is this really you, covered in that veil?
Am I hallucinating, or is it just my fear?
Frozen feet, my eyes at front, a cold breath following my rear

A SECRET

Let me tell you a secret
A secret like a nuclear reactor
The radius is about to blow
A secret so dark and cold
It will crumble your families' kingdom
Your king on his knees, eyes on the ground look at him bow

I apologize if it hurts you
But the justice has been done
Consequences are aligned in place
The leadership is undone

Let me tell you a secret
A secret that acts on its own
Been so long in hiding
Finally, the truth reveals, mask removed
Your Leader has been thrown